<u>Tainted Prayers</u>

<u>*A Narrative in Verse*</u>

This is a work of fiction. Similarities to real people, places, or events are entirely coincidental.

TAINTED PRAYERS

First edition. October 6, 2023.

Copyright © 2023 Dare Edwards.

ISBN: 979-8223763109

Written by Dare Edwards.

To those who have let the darkness seep in. To those who were forced to accept it.

Author's Note

The story of *Tainted Prayers* is my take on a cosmic horror/dark fantasy tale. While there are overt religious (namely Christianity) references and themes interspersed throughout this narrative it should not be taken as an approval (nor a condemnation) of Christianity or an overtly Christian text.

There are two major players in this narrative: the entity of *Darkness* and his vessel Pastor James.

As a sign of veneration to the cosmic creator, *Darkness (it/he/him),* any mention of it will be italicized as will any part of the *Darkness's* own narrative. *Darkness* and his creation will be seen in the first section entitled, Origin. *Darkness* reigns over a pantheon of other mythological entities. He has just as much influence upon the cosmos, which he created, as he does on human beings.

One such being is our main character, Pastor James who we first meet as a child where he first encounters the *Darkness* after being sexually abused by both his mother, his mother's boyfriends and his priest. This act opens James up to the darkness and we follow him as he descends further into it.

Note: Pastor James first appeared in the narrative *frankie is a junkie whore.*

Tainted Prayers is all about giving into those dark cravings that rumble deep within our gut, deep within our soul. It won't hurt to give into the *darkness. He* is always there, always present. He knows your name and knows your voice, he is only waiting for your call.

Content Warnings: *Tainted Prayers* includes subjects that some readers may find offensive such as but not limited to: sexual assault, molestation, cannibalism, religious abuse, Christian rites (such as Communion), murder, fetal death, drug abuse, implications of rape and sexual assault.

Tainted Prayers

Origin

At the beginning there was only Darkness
It reigned over the Nothingness
All was blanketed in its boundless blackness
Silence filled the endless emptiness,
The timeless space
And all within Darkness was in order
Darkness, the primordial deity,
Had one child, Umbra, which maintained this order
And from Darkness emerged the Cosmos
And all were within Darkness
And all were in order
Yet by cosmic chance
Chaos too sprung from Darkness
Burning bright
Piercing the dark shroud
Pouring out the blinding anti-darkness, Light
Through Umbra came its weaker offspring
Shadows to combat Chaos' Light
But the cosmic blunder had already disrupted the order within the cosmos
Splitting the Darkness
Light brought forth the Day
Shadows brought the Night
Beginning a struggle without end
Since this cosmic treason
Chaos and Darkness
Have remained in constant battle
Darkness ruled over the Night
Chaos, the Day
Light quickly spread across the universe
Yet never has it successfully drowned out Shadows in totality

DARE EDWARDS

Darkness has made its strides
Greatly overtaking Chaos and Light
Through the cosmic act known as Eclipse
Temporarily restoring order back to the Cosmos
Chaos' greatest stride
Was made within the Shadows of Darkness
Birthing something even more vile, Life
Since Chaos only had Dark-matter to work with
Its creations were all fabricated from Darkness
Cut from the same dark cloth
But bound in Light
The Darkness within these "light-beings"
Eventually eclipsed their illumination
Leading to their Death (or return to Darkness)
This internal conflict of Life
Has led to external conflict within
What is now known as the Human race
Darkness remains ruler of the Cosmos
Influencing and intervening in the lives of light-beings
Who wish to give into their own darkness
And return to their original state of being
However, the Human race has proved
Beneficial to both Darkness and Chaos
As it freely participates in both its reproduction and its destruction
Though Chaos allows its light-beings
To freely evolve and devolve
The Darkness, omniscient, knows even Death is living
The Darkness, attentive, is always listening
For those who call

Part I

In the beginning there was Darkness
And the Darkness was with god
And the Darkness was god

A Mother's Love (I)

I knew her body
Before I knew mine
Nine months
She held me
Growing inside
She held on for
One hundred sixty-two more
Each night
That she took my body
Cold intentions
Yet warm hands
And I grew inside
Should a mother's love
Be this deep?
Familiarizing myself
With a road only once traveled
A secret held under covers
Should this be kept undercover?
No, not the love of a mother
I tasted the whiskey on her lips
Her tainted words, *give us a kiss*
From my neck
She continued down
And it felt good
And I hated that
But she was, after all, my mother
And mothers know best
And I couldn't let her down
She knows my body
So too do I know hers

TAINTED PRAYERS

This just might be
This unconditional love of a mother

Confession (I)

Forgive me, Father, for I have sinned
I thought I could trust him
But he asked the same question
Knowing I was trusting
Can you keep a secret?
This was meant to be my confession
He was meant to be my savior
Yet here I am
Perverting this sacrament
Perhaps this is my penance
For being so broken
Establishing this covenant
with a holy man
He felt good, he felt right
But I'm not meant to lie by his side
But I'd be lying to myself
To deny him
After never having denied her sin
Nor my own
It may be wrong
But it can't be
At least that is what he tells me
Because it feels so right
Daily scriptures, daily lessons
Taught from church to home
He tells me it's our secret
My confession
He is my penance
But with him
I am not penitent

TAINTED PRAYERS

This holy man
With worldly ways
His are mysterious
This is life
The truth
The only way

A Mother's Love (II)

Her love has become rougher
Sourced from the bottom of brown bottles
She slides in undercovers
But tonight it is not just her
These hands are bigger, tougher
I guess, I am no longer momma's boy
Give us a kiss
His voice is tainted
Just like hers
He insists he's going to be my new father
One thousand ninety-five nights
They laid by my side
Entering underneath the darkness of night
Reassuring, that this was all right
I knew his body
And he knew mine
I cannot confess this sin away
The Father listens
But there are not enough words to pray
He stills sends me to my knees
My mouth is no longer of use
Unless it is being used to please
The angles of this triangle
Sharpened, intent to mangle
But there is another here
I cannot see *him*
But I feel *him*
Not like the others
Deeper as if in my blood
Deeper as if it is one with the darkness

TAINTED PRAYERS

I do not know what this feeling is
But I hope it never goes

darkness calls out

You poor thing
I see pieces of me in you
Can you see pieces of yourself in me?
How does such a lovely flower
Grow in a darkened
Dry garden
I only wish to help you
Do you not know
To every thing there is a season
Even for that which escapes our understanding
There is a reason
For every ebb
So too must there be a flow
And it is infinite
Always moving
No matter how fast or slow it goes
You precious thing
For us to return to death
We first must undergo birth
To truly understand and appreciate the darkness
We must suffer the light and its burn
We laugh
So too must we weep
We sow
So we must reap
We hunger
So we must feed
And I know how to sate
Those painful cravings
I see your dark dreams

TAINTED PRAYERS

Let me color them for you
I know it can be terrifying
But you need not fear me
Yes, bad things can happen in the dark
But in me, you need not fret
Nothing bad will come upon you
I only wish to give thee the treasures of the darkness
I can show you
The darkness within
I already see it in you
You only have to let me in
I can take away the false prophets
I can take away their sin
You sweet thing
You and I know
In time our hurt will mend
So too do we know
That time takes its precious time to begin healing
You sweet thing
Let me heal you
Tell me thy name
James
Give me your hand

a darker love

In her hands
Is where I found you
Where you sought protection
The hands meant to mend you
Only left you broken
That is where I found you
Through the cracks
I seeped in
Through your cracks
You let me in
Did you feel me?
Or were those grown hands too rough
Traveling under the cover of night
Undercover
She gave you life
She gave you your name
But with each night
Unprotected, under a dim nightlight
She dwindled your life away
How many nights did that door creak open?
How many nights did you fear that sound?
When she let those men
Let themselves in
How many nights
Did she slip in
Whiskey on her breath
Her mind focused on sin?
Her darkness
Was an opening
Your fear

TAINTED PRAYERS

Your hate
Beckoned me in
I heard you, calling
Even though not even you were aware you were inviting
I saw the silver in your eyes
I knew you heard me
How could a woman forget her nursing child?
To let rot
The fruit of her womb?
Even those who may forget
I will never forget you
You felt me
In you
The first cut will always be the most deep
Yet you pulled me in deeper
As you gave deeper
Into me
I will help you
I am the way
I will set you free

Confession (II)

I feel *him* enter me
Not in the way the others did
As if I too am entering *him*
I tasted *him*
Not bitter like other men
Yet *he* is not man
He is something more
Instinct tells me this
The only thing of which I am sure
He speaks to me
He understands
He wishes to guide me
Asking for very little
Compared to what *he* has to give
He is there
Surrounding me
Mending me
After they're done breaking
He's with me
Guiding me
Down the street
Knife in hand
Through those oak doors
I kneel before him
As I've done countless times before
And I enter him
But not in the way he entered me
I feel his warmth
Sticky and sweet
Blanket me

TAINTED PRAYERS

He loves this
The darkening of my skin
The deeper the blade goes
The deeper *he* lets himself in
My final confession
Forgive me Father
As I have forgiven you and your trespasses
This is your penance
I am no longer penitent
For your sin

...

The priest's death
A shrouded in darkness
As I was
Years leave
Days linger
Seven hundred thirty
For each, I delved deeper
So too did *he*
I did not fight
His euphoric touch
Though *he* was rough
He was the first to hold me
And it not hurt
Fire coursing through my veins
I felt *him* making space
Replacing the breath in my lungs
The thoughts in my brain
He enters me
Bit by bit
Filling me
Taking all of what I was with *him*

Until I am just as empty as *he* is
I did not fight
I wouldn't want to
If I could
And I couldn't if I tried
He filled me
Showing me a reality
I never knew I was missing
He only asked
For a taste of iron
To make them bleed and
Mine were perpetually heated
He knew my cravings
And only wanted to satisfy
He knew my dreams
And only wanted to bring them to life
I was calling
Never believing anyone was listening
He called me
Welcoming me sweetly
I couldn't help but give into the *darkness*

A Mother's Love (III)

As the nights become darker
The bedroom door still creaking open
My blade soon finds home in her
I filled her
As I once did
Only this time
Different
She did not moan
She screamed
But not for more
That night was the last
Of that creaking door
As the blade slashed
Guided by *his* hand
The body
I've known
That has known me
Which gave me life
Darkens
The wounds deepen
Inch by jagged inch
Creating a new body
Erasing the sin
As her blood flows
I wonder
Where will the love go?
...
She has given
Her life for your own
This is the depth of a mother's love

DARE EDWARDS

This was how it was always meant to end

darkness sets in

You are mine
Do not deny me
But to be mine
You must deny yourself
Of this flesh
You have tainted
You are not this body nor this blood
Give it to me
Let me in
Say you belong to me
What you do
You do for me
And I will do for you
Give into me
And I'll give unto you
...
Do you feel me
Wriggling within
Slithering
Beneath the skin
It is no longer of any use
Give to me thy walking corpse
Let me rid you of this unnatural anatomy
Meet me
Where five streams become one
Travel down the river
They will all reach the ocean
Though the sea
Never fills
Open those gates

DARE EDWARDS

And let it spill
I know it is constricting
But you do not need to breathe
I will be your airway
Allow me space
I will fit right in
Allow me to stretch
And fill what's underneath the skin
Pushing aside
Heart and brain
Simple clusters of the dust
From whence you came
You have no need for them
You only need to let me in
Tendons snap
Bones crack
I know it's rough
But do not fight it
This is love
Overtaking
Take it in
Feel the warmth
Surrounding
As I set fire to this frame
Feel the blood boil
Evaporating in the vein
I know it's painful
But feel the pain, inflammatory
As you become bone of my bone
Restoration; replacing your flesh with my own
Even Death knows it is living
You need not give anymore

TAINTED PRAYERS

You need only to give in
Feel me fill you
Entering
As you invited me
I welcome you
To enter me

...

I feel *him*
In me as I am in *him*
He is completely within me
And with *him*, I am complete

Part II

If I wait, the grave is mine house: I have made my bed in darkness.
- Job 17:13
The darkness was made flesh
and dwelt among us

Return

Sometimes when I am all alone
I think of home
Walls, built up
Easy to take down
But *he* is a fortress
Unshakeable
A burning fire
Never dying
I am impermanent
I am only a product of *his* making
Every time
Their blood spills
I feel *him* deeply
As *he* fills me deeply
Reaffirming our covenant
Through this offering
Every time
Is a homecoming
A return?
I never left
And *he's* never left me

Return (II)

This is where I found you
The light had already dimmed
Let me put it out, it was only ever in the way
I heard your call
You heard mine just the same
Give to me
Thy body and blood
And I will give to you
The gift of a living shadow
I see you
Where others look over
I've heard your hunger pains
Do not deny yourself
For the longer you starve
The darker your cravings become
And the deeper your pain
This is my offering
Should you give to me
I will satiate
A return?
You have never left
And you never have to leave

The Calling

Keep calling
They all do
But no one will answer
No one will hear you
...
He has carried me
My shelter
My covering
I find myself in a strange land
And yet in a familiar place
Forgive me, Father
For I have sinned
This is my first confession
In this city of sin
I have come far from home
There was nowhere else to go
Out on my own
Only wishing to begin again
And so I did
With *him*
Taking the holy disguise
Of many worldly men
This was my calling
They call me by my official name
Pastor James
Cross dangling from my neck
Rhythmically hitting their chin
They stop calling
Their eyes glossy
Their understanding enlightened

DARE EDWARDS

They now know the riches of the glory of *him*
The hope of *his* calling
As they give into me
Just as I gave into *him*

Living Shadow (I)

Who knew there could be such comfort
In obscurity
In the darkness
In *him?*
Sunday mornings
As dark as childhood nights
He told me this was the way
To hide in plain sight
And now I know
How it is
To exist
Only as a shadow
Amongst the darkness
He is in me
And I in *him*
I have seen a time
Before time began
I listen
As they repent
He has led me
To the underbelly of society
They trust me
They see me
I lie, they lay
But they see me
As the way
And I am the way
I am the light
Though a shadow
This is the truth

This is life
I cannot save them all
For we were all foredoomed
But I can brace their fall
No matter how venial
They do not know
That I walk among them
That they venerate mortal sin
That they feed my carnal cravings
Though when they fall into my hands
They never retreat
They need to be redeemed
Always in the need of saving
But they cannot be blamed
For it is always sweet
When the darkness calls our name
And welcomes us in

The Calling (II)

This was my offering
He heard me calling
And offered
The ability to be a shadow
Among the living
All I had to do was
Give *him* an offering
He has guided me
Taught me to express
The darkness
Inside of me
And he sees it in my eyes
As I see his darken
He's letting me in
Even though he is still squirming
It only makes me harder
Their cries, reaffirming
Imbibe
As their blood spills, rains
Take all of them
As they take all of me in
Drunk off their pain
Keep calling
They all do
But no one will answer
No one will hear you
This is darkness calling
You heard me
A fool for answering

The Body

Flesh
That is all this is
It is there
For me to rid it
Of its impurities
To cleanse it
Completely
Flesh
But it is more than that
What lovely tastes come
With such little fat

...

Their body
A clean canvas
Simply asking
To be perverted
By slashes of color
To be converted
Into an absence
Into a sum, negative
They all cry out
But what good will that do?
They all want to know why
I cannot be blamed
For what they've made me do
Look how you gave in so easily
I will take every inch of flesh
Each piece of you, broken bread
This is your offering
This is bigger than you

Give into me
Give into *him*

31

The Blood

With each piece of flesh
And each sip
Taken
I needed more
He filled my cup
And it runneth over
Too much of *him*
Was never enough
Each offering
Brings *him* closer to me
I've never known
Anyone this deeply
I need *him*
So I will follow *him*
Wherever he leads
I began to enjoy it
Just to be around *him*
So I will do
Whatever *he* needs
Whatever *he* desires
For *he* is my deepest one
Their taste, bitter
But the more I imbibe
The sweeter they become
...
This is our covenant
Poured out
Give them to me
I will give unto you

The Body (II)

We cannot be blamed
For what you made us do
We saw your dying light
It was inviting
Do not deny yourself
The darkness is what you truly want
What you truly need
Your eyes
Your laugh
Your lips
They all let us in
You cannot deny us
There is no alternative
You have already denied the light
It is time you fully give in
Do not try to fight us now
Each piece of you
Bound to be broken
Eventually
We are your penance
You are the offering
...
Take this body
This flesh
Broken
In remembrance of me

The Body and the Blood

You are more than this body
You are more than your blood
You have given yourself to me
You are more than the clod from whence you come
Above all
You are a part of me
I who ascends above the heights of the clouds
And below the depths of the sea
For I was before both the heavens
And the oceans
I, before everything
You are greater now
You have given
And you have taken
Thy body and thy blood
Replenished
By their flesh
Restored
By their blood
You are greater than
You are more than tainted blood
More than fetid flesh
You are greater than
For you are a part of me

Part III

There is a way which seemeth right unto a man,
but the end thereof are the ways of death.
- Proverbs 14:13
It is a faithful saying: For if we be dead with him, we shall also live with
him
If we suffer, we shall also reign with him:
if we deny him, he also will deny us
- 2 Timothy 2:11-12

Umbra (Interlude)

How transforming it is
To be one with him
He shows me more
Than minds could conceive
He exists within me
And I within him
Guiding me
Through him I am free
I am their judgment
I am their penance
They, my offering
I will lay the nations low
I now see in his way
I am more than a living shadow
I am the darkness
I am one with him
I am greater than

Unworthy (A Mother's Love IV)

How can you bring life
When you do not have what it takes to survive?
Your pain in labor
Will be nothing compared to its hunger
It hungers for your touch
For your love
Is it asking too much
Of you to be a mother
Instead of the fucker that you are?
You inject your veins
To erase your pain
Inflicting it onto another
Do you not hear the cries
Echoing inside you
Or can your hollow hole
Only be fulfilled
With men
Who fill you with
Lethal blends
Do you not feel it kick?
Do you not feel for shit?
Or do you just need another hit?
Well here is a final dose
And it will be the greatest high of your life
When you let my darkness in

Hallowed: a haiku

Two distinct cries, screams
Each sent off with a slit, rip
One hole dug for two

Blind (or In Darkness)

She wakes up
Bright and fresh
She heads to her closet
Because she wants to look her best
She goes through her clothes
This shirt isn't what she's feeling
She wants something tight and loud
She wants something short and revealing
She finds the perfect outfit
The one that says "easy"
The one that says "feel me"
She's already asking for it
Because her outfit is consenting
So she should not fight
When you are only answering
She heads to the mirror
Because pallor is not a good color
Concealer is more than concealing
For someone who wants to break
Who wants to be broken
Her lips painted a bright red
The color is simply inviting
She is searching for something
She just doesn't know it's me
Her made up skin,
Revealing flesh,
Revealing her consent
That's all she is
I will take her
I will make her give in

DARE EDWARDS

She's walking home
Quick, before she gets in
My foot stops the door
And I invite myself in
In reality, she offered the invitation
With those red lips
And those visible thighs
Her hair, long and flowing
Dipping into her exposed breasts
She wanted it all right
She runs
But she cannot hide
And why deprive her
Of something she truly wanted
She's crying but it is okay
Because she wanted this
She didn't say it, she didn't have to
She didn't need words
Because she conveyed it
She asked for this
I was only the answer
The light had already dimmed
There was no other choice
But for her to give in

The junkie whore (Frankie I)

They are all the same
Showing what they could offer me
But he is different
Nevertheless, he is just another offering
I have tasted the body of god
And that of his son
I have drank the blood
Not only does my cup runneth over
It floods
His eyes wide
But I can see there is a light inside
He wishes to remain in the dark
But I see them for what they are
This is the longest I've waited for one
But I know it will be worth it
I can smell the Life
Underneath the pain, semen and chem piss
He smells sweet
Like lavender
I bet he'll taste even sweeter
He doesn't know
But he will be the best I've ever had
For he will be all mine
I've been watching him
In the darkness
Even as he walks amongst the shadows
His is already fading
A shell of his former self
But I can see within his darkness
The boy who wishes to escape this hell

DARE EDWARDS

He's leaving
He's swaying
As he enters the drugstore
I watch from a distance
He's popped some pills into his mouth
Maybe red, maybe blue
Not sure what they are
But they do what he needs them to
Falling into a pile of his own mess
I call out, distressed
What's your name?
Frankie
I'm Pastor James...

Stop (I)

Stop
I can hear his voice
As if coming through a haze
As if he's not here
But faraway
In some distant place
But he's not, he is here
Right here, in my hands
Stop
Does he hear me?
Does he understand my command
Even coated with the darkness
Of my intentions?
Stop
His tears wet my hands
His breath is strained
In my grip
Stop
He doesn't say it but
I see it in his bloodshot eyes
The awareness

    The darkness creeping in

He must see it in mine

He has stopped fighting
There was never that much in him
To begin with
But he must feel it

That's why he's stopped
Why he's given in
Stop
But I cannot
I've not had enough
Though that is enough for him

X (Frankie's Interlude I)

Once again
Here I am
In a stranger's bed
But he's different
At least he feels different
I hope I'm not wrong
But I always end up right
In the wrong place, wrong time
I didn't even drink that much
But we all know
How I get with that sweetness
On my lips
My problem
Always thinking problems
Can be solved
If you search deep within
A bottle or two
It's a rational thought
Even if you thought you were fine
Even if you were told
Never mix, never worry
Even though mixing
Takes away the worries
That last shot was probably
My one too many
Because I am tight in his hands
But different than I've ever been
Well would you look at that
He was different after all
And once again here I am

DARE EDWARDS

In the bed of a stranger
My resting place forever
As the darkness sets in

46

Hopeful (Frankie II)

He was too easy
He gave in so quickly
For something as weak
As a confession of love
After all the drugs
And all the men
Love
Or the hope for it
Is what would do him in
There is no fight
There is no life
Left in him
He is mine
He knows that
It's reflected in his glassy eyes
But even still he reaches for me
He truly believed
"Frankie, sweet Frankie
Don't fight
It's useless
I was always the way
This was always the way it would end
Frankie, sweet Frankie
Thank you for your offering."

Final Light (Frankie's Interlude II)

There's light outside my window
But I'm stuck on the inside
Looking down on myself
As above they fly
Settling on my flesh
As he takes and takes
Until I'm nothing but scraps
Of who I am, of who I had ever been
They look down
They're looking down on me
They just don't know I'm kept down here
I have always been kept secret
Do they know what it's like inside?
Do they hear me down here
Do they hear my cries?
There's light outside
But my room is drowning in darkness
My world is void of light
What a fool to think this was my life?
Darkness
It's always calling
I haven't the voice to say no
I thought that this was meant to be
That this time maybe it'd be my time
That this was mine
But none of this is
Not even this name
Because he's staked his claim
I am nothing more
Than an offering

pieces of me (Frankie's Interlude III)

He said I was sweet
And he would be my escape
There was some kind of peace
Of not belonging to anyone
But being wanted by everyone
Even though I was never alone
I was always lonely
He was meant to be my escape
But he wasn't as sweet
As he said I was
There is no peace
In knowing I'm not whole
Not wholly enough for anyone
Because everyone
Only wants a piece
Do they remember me there?
Because my body is missing
The pieces of me
I left behind
The pieces that he now consumes
Yet somehow I'm comfortable
Tossing and turning
That wrenching deep in the gut
At least, for once, I am enough

Living Shadow (II)

I hear him
He is calling
He is searching
He's found himself
Lost in my web
He's already a living shadow
He's already let the darkness in
Through every orifice and vein
It's deep in him
But there is something wrong here
He does not belong here
He is not the same
He's calling out
For Tony, for J
Approaching him
Tell me thy name
Frankie
There is no need to fight
You need not fear me
Should you welcome me in
I, too, welcome you sweetly
I will not hurt you any more
Than what you have already endured
Frankie, do not fear me
For within me you are free
You are greater than you know
More than just a living shadow
I see those pieces of you
I can make you whole
I am more than you can even begin to imagine

TAINTED PRAYERS

I am much more than even he knows

Part IV

He discovereth deep things out of darkness
and bringeth out to light the shadow of death.
- Job 12:22
In the beginning there was only Darkness
And so too at the end
Darkness is all there is

Disorder

Within Darkness
There was disorder
And this time not due in part
To the cosmic mishap, Chaos
This disorder was brought forth
From within the darkness itself
By one of his own disciples
A waning shadow
Living amongst shadows
Who had forgotten its place
Sights on ascension
Beyond the depths
Of darkness itself
This worldly man
In holy disguise
How foolish man can be
But there is no deceiving
Obscurity

Welcome

Sweet Frankie
Your flesh is weak
Then again all flesh is
But your spirit is willing
Even in Death
I could hear it calling
I cannot return you to life
But I can make you a part of something greater than
Greater than life, than man
Which was never that great
To begin with
There is a darkness in you
I've heard the rumble
Always in search of someone
Intent on saving
And you have found yourself here
And I have found you
Living amongst the shadows
So be not afraid
To rejoin them
Do not fear the darkness
Do not fear death
For many Death is stagnant
Simply a conclusion
But I see more in you Frankie
This is not an end
But only where it all begins
I want you here
I reached out for his hand
And he flinched back

TAINTED PRAYERS

As if I were made of fire
Ages passed
Before he reached back
And held on
As if it were for the first time
He was touched
And he wasn't burned
Frankie
Take my hand
You are safe here

The Body (II)

He feels it
Weighing heavy within him
His breaths stagger
His heart which once
Beat in tune with a dark rhythm
Skips
Something is wrong
It is *darkness*
But now it is deeper
Than it's even been
...
You foolish man
You have forgotten
Flesh
That is all this is
That is all you are
I cannot be blamed
For what you have brought onto yourself
Your dying light
Invited me in
I have given unto you
Because I found you
Enshadowed in darkness
I only wished to let you in
Flesh
Is all I asked in return
You have tainted it
And its bitter taste burns
You are no better
Than the impurities

TAINTED PRAYERS

You have cloyingly gratified
Your hunger with
You have been gluttonous
Continuing to feed
Indulging excessively
Even after you had your fill
You have been covetous
You blaspheme
My presence
Claiming you and I
Are one and the same
Of one substance
But what you have forgotten
Is that you
A shadow amongst Darkness
Are made
Not begotten
Neglectful of what is within you
You have become
Just as tainted
As the flesh you consume
Scraps of humanity
Yet void of what consumes you
And it is I
Or have you forgotten
How dare you claim to be my iron rod
When your lustful flames
Have melted thy very core
You are not the darkness
I have filled you with
You are but the shadow
Of a shadow

You do not shatter flesh and blood
That is my work through you
You cannot separate brain and heart
Nor heaven and earth
You cannot without me
But I can without you
I was here before the light
I was here before she slipped in
Before she opened you up to me
I am the only true way
Because without me
You are nothing more
I have not forsaken you
You have brought this expulsion upon yourself
Do not deny this
As you have denied me
Do not fight this
There is no use fighting
"Give unto me
As I give into you"
But you cannot take back
As I take it all back from you
Each piece
Bound to be broken
Bound to the darkness
I am your penance
This is your final offering

The Blood (II)

The warmth that once filled him
Ran cold through his tainted blood
Just as quickly as the darkness entered him
So too did it leave
He had never felt an emptiness such as this
This weakness
Weighed heavy in his mind
And solid in his gut
The warmth has left him
He has never been this cold
His hunger returns
He has never had a craving this deep
His mind races
He reaches out
Into the void
But the void turns away
Plunged into a nothingness
Painfully aware
On a plane
Between death and non-existence
An unmoving
Unwavering
Unconscious
Conscience
Where once the darkness
Had filled him with emptiness
The emptiness he now felt
Was only a brutal reminder
Of his own nothingness
A dying shadow under fading light

DARE EDWARDS

Just as a memory exists at the end of time
Utterly forgotten

Return (II)

Sometimes when I am all alone
I think of home
Walls, built up
Easy to take down
But *he* is a fortress
Unescapable
His undying fire
No longer warms me
Not heeding
His warning
I am impermanent
Only a product of his making
My blood spilling
I feel him leaving
Where I once felt him so deeply
Our covenant broken
Of my own doing
Once
A homecoming
This return
Is not welcoming
How foolish
To rebuke the air I breathe
I left him
I accept why he has left me

The Body and the Blood (II)

Sometimes when I am alone
I think of home
However, here within this darkness
This endless emptiness
I am not alone
They have been waiting for me
I hear their cries
Their screams
They're calling
Welcoming me
Tattered faces
Shattered souls
Consumed corpses
Regurgitated, reanimated
The ones I hungered for
Now wish to feed on me
I see her
Ahead of the others
Their blood spilling
Was an act of consecration
Now it is only my own
Meant to atone
I am within the darkness
But *he* is no longer within me
They take my body
And my blood
Strip me of my skin
Break me of my skeleton
And they take of me
My final communion

Stop (II)

Stop
He has stopped calling
He knows I will not answer
Stop
Does he still feel me here?
I still feel his fear
I still hear the mashing of their jaws
Denying nature's laws
Those dark cravings
Rumble still

They are still feeding

They are the hardest to fill
Stop
Though I will not
I, without end,
I have not had enough
Though that is enough for him

Order: a haiku

There is once again
Order within the Darkness
Nothing left, only darkness

Return (III)

Though my existence
As a shroud of darkness
Though I am nothingness
I am not nonexistent
Nor am I void
Of self-reflection
All comes from me
So too does all return
But truly
I feel as if a part of me
Has atrophied
The phantom limb
Of a body that will endlessly yearn
There was a beacon in the darkness
But that light has dimmed
Even I knew, it was over
Before it could ever begin

Afterword

I began *Tainted Prayers* because after finishing my first narrative in verse, *frankie is a junkie whore,* I truly was not ready to let Frankie and the world he inhabited go. With this writing I believe I was finally able to lay him to rest.

I would highly recommend you read both works, in no particular order.

As well, I wanted to explore the concept of "darkness" as an entity. This evolved from a simple story of a serial killer pastor to a man who was an agent of a lost god.

As I said at the top in my Author's Note, I am not a religious person. I was raised in the Christian church so that is the religion I am most familiar with and that experience is what I sprinkled throughout these pages.

While I am not religious, I believe this freedom from theism allowed me to bend and mend and cherry-pick (as Christians often do) scripture, luckily for me there were hundreds of verses that directly referenced "darkness" to choose from.

This work is not to be a condemnation of Christianity (although that may be a personal belief) but it was my way of discussing the often hypocritical nature of those who purport to be followers of Jesus Christ, the ole failed apocalyptic prophet himself.

If you have made it this far, I want to thank you for joining me on this ride of creation and destruction.

About the Author

Dare Edwards is an active agent of the Darkness. He pledges his sole allegiance to the lost god. Through the darkness, he has written two short horror story collections: *darker cravings* and *Tales of a Dark Dreamer*. In addition, his first narrative in verse, *frankie is a junkie whore*, was met with rave reviews (mainly from his friends).

He is comfortable in darkness and the darkness is a comfort within him. He patiently awaits his final return to darkness. Until then he writes.

Twitter: @darkdreamerdare

TikTok: @darklydreamingdare